Inspired by True Events

REMINISCENCE

Book 1

Alayshia

All rights reserved. No part of this book/publication may be reproduced, stored in a retrieval system, or transmitted in any form or by any means, electronic, mechanical, photocopying, recording, or otherwise; without written consent from both the author and publisher of Exposed Books Publishing, LLC, except for brief quotes used in reviews. The text inside of this book has been copyrighted. Any references to real people or real places are used fictitiously. Names, characters, and places are products of the author's imagination or used in a fictitious manner. For information regarding special discounts or bulk purchases, please contact Alayshia Adams at info@readreminiscence.com or Exposed Books Publishing at info@exposedbooks.com.

© 2020, by Alayshia Adams and Exposed Books Publishing, LLC
All rights reserved, including the right of reproduction in whole or in part of any form.
ISBN 978-1-7361999-3-0
Library of Congress Number 2021900766
Reminiscence
www.readreminiscence.com
Written by: Alayshia Adams
Printed in the United States of America

Chapter 1

"Wake up, Ava! Amir is dead!" Yves screamed as he swung open the bedroom door to find Ava stirring from sleep. That day changed Ava's life forever.

***

It was 2:30 pm on an ordinary Tuesday in October. Ava sat outside the house Amir had been hustling from for the past few months. He ran his business a few blocks down where one of his homeboys stayed.

"Bro, I'm outside," Ava informed Amir. "Alright, here I come, sis."

Within moments, Amir appeared from the back of the house. He was of average height and thin. His handsome, clean-shaven face made him quite the ladies' man. He wore a white t-shirt and jeans. He was always fitted, but he was looking thinner, even from a

1

distance. *"If Remy were still here, she would make sure he was eating good,"* Ava thought silently, missing her childhood friend.

Today, she was there to pick up a sack before her three to eleven shift at a residential facility. Ava knew she had to catch Amir before she started work because she did not want to be out late. That, and he was often hard to catch up with as the night went on.

Amir opened Ava's car door and eased inside. The two of them sat and talked as Amir handed Ava the little tied-off sandwich bag of weed.

"You need to get off this street," Ava warned. "You don't need to be down here. What do I keep telling you?" she continued. Ava always had her reservations about Amir's line of work.

"Sis, it's okay," he said with a sigh. Everyone was always so concerned. "It's just smoke," he said. "It's not like I'm out here selling hard and got crackheads running through," he defended himself.

"Do you at least have a gun with you?" Ava questioned.

"Yes," he responded.

"Alright, then. Don't stay down here all day," Ava demanded.

"I'm not. I'm going home in a lil bit," he stated.

"You're off tomorrow. I'm going to come kick it with you and bro," Amir told Ava.

"Okay, cool," Ava smiled, easing her stern face just a little. "I love you," Ava said as she pulled away from the corner house, not realizing that was the last time she would see Amir alive.

"Love and Hip Hop is coming on tonight," said one of Ava's co-workers. Ava looked at her watch. It was close to 8:30 p.m. Typically, Ava and Tameka would have the meds and dinner done for the residents in enough time to watch their favorite primetime shows. On this particular night, Ava had an unexplained sense of agitation that prevented her from turning the TV on. She did not feel sick and was fairly certain that she did not have food poisoning. It was more of a restless unease that she could not explain. As the time drew closer to 11 pm, Ava's phone started ringing. She thought nothing of it and switched the phone off. Her friends knew she could not answer when she was at work. Filled with an underlying anger, Ava drove straight home and went right to bed when her shift was over.

The following morning, Ava's eyes fluttered open at the sound of Yves's feet racing up the stairs. He turned on the light in their bedroom and yelled with urgency, "Wake up, Ava! Amir is dead!" His fingers scrambled for the remote, shaking as he fumbled with the buttons to turn on the local news.

Ava sat up, startled. "What do you mean?" Ava's heart began to race as she tried to clear the fog from her head.

"Look!" Yves instructed, pointing to the TV. Ava's blood started to run cold as she watched the Channel 11 Wake Up News. "Twenty-Five-year-old Amir Wailon Davis was shot and killed last night in the neighborhood of..." the reporter informed viewers.

Ava's vision crossed. She tried to stand but fell to her trembling knees. She started to scream in disbelief. "Noooo!" she cried, gasping for air. "This is not happening! I just saw him yesterday!"

Ava grabbed her phone from the nightstand and pushed the power button. It had been off since last night. Messages and voicemails began to light up her phone, but Ava swiped the notifications away to call her mom. "He's dead, mom! They killed him!" Ava started to scream, half choking on her grief, when her mom, Patrice, answered.

"Who's dead!?" Patrice questioned. "Yves?" she said with confusion, trying to follow Ava's jumbled speech. "What! What? Yves is dead?" her mother continued.

"No! Mom, its Amir!" Ava screamed. Yves grabbed the phone from Ava and put it to his ear. He was more composed than Ava, but not by much. "No. It's me. I'm okay. Amir got shot last night; turn on the news," Yves instructed. There was a pause, followed by a sharp gasp and pained screams on the other line. The sound sent Ava into a crying fit once again. The entire neighborhood loved Amir. What kind of person could take it upon themselves to end his life?

After Ava and her mom got off the phone, she started to shift through her messages when Keisha called. She was one of the people who left Ava multiple voicemails.

"I was calling you last night to tell you. I was trying to tell you before you woke up and saw it on the news," Keisha said with a shaky voice.

"I'm just seeing it right now," Ava responded.

"Are you going to call Remy?" Keisha asked. Ava's heart dropped. At this point, her best friend and mother of Amir's child lived in North Carolina.

"Yes," Ava managed to whisper as her throat seemed to swell up with grief, rendering her nearly unable to speak.

Ava looked at her contact list and scrolled to the R's. She took a deep breath, never thinking in a million years that she would have to call her best friend from five hundred miles away to tell her that the father of their three-year-old girl was murdered the night before. Ava pressed the call button and looked at the clock. It was still only 6:23 am.

"Ava? What's up, girl? Its early," Remy said, sounding like she just woke up. Ava swallowed the lump that was crawling up her throat.

"Remy," Ava said, pausing to take a breath.

"What's wrong, Ava?" Remy asked, hearing the despair in Ava's voice.

"Remy... I am so, so sorry..." Ava started again. "Remy, somebody shot Amir last night. He didn't survive. He's gone, Remy."

Ava's heart throbbed when she heard the singular, shrill scream come from the other end of the line. Ava felt so terrible that Remy was so far away from her biggest support system. The two sat crying on the phone, neither able to speak. "I love you," Ava whispered gently. "I am about to go down to Grams'. I'll see you when you get here."

When Ava got to Grams' house, just blocks away from where Amir took his last breath, there was already a large crowd that formed, despite it being early in the morning. She spoke with his mom and brothers before going around the corner to Akhi's Market. Amir and Ava were close friends with Rico, one of the owners. Rico told Ava he saw Amir right before he died. The two were talking and joking like always.

"Did anything seem out of the ordinary?" Ava asked, thinking maybe Amir got into an argument with someone.

"Not at all," Rico replied. "It was like an ordinary day. I can't believe how crazy this all is. I am so sorry, sis."

Ava sat in her car outside of the market and lit up. Calls started pouring in from people offering condolences and speculating on who might have killed Amir. *It might have been this person. It might have been that person,* they would say. Ava was suspicious of everyone. She took the small, pink handgun from her glove compartment and put it on her passenger seat.

Chapter 2

2001 was a memorable year. The movie Ocean's Eleven just came out, the world's longest train was built in Australia, George W. Bush became president, and the average cost of gas was $1.46. It was also the year my mom, my sister, and I moved to Wilkinsburg, Pennsylvania. I was ready for the next adventure to begin. We had been staying at Mother's house in Point Breeze. Both my brother and I called our grandmother, "Mother." Although we moved around every few years, living in places like Penn Hills and Lincoln Larimer, her house was like home base. No matter what neighborhood we moved to, going back to Mother's house on Penfield Court was always an option.

Our rooms remained untouched in our absence. My mom and Brielle stayed in the basement that was set up like an apartment, while Vonte and I had our own bedrooms upstairs, and Mother slept in the living room.

My brother was the least social of us, and because he had issues with his dad, he tended to stay with Mother in the interest of comfort and stability as my mom, sister, and I moved around. Knowing we had a home base gave me a sense of security that I am thankful for to this day. Besides, we were never too far away. Wilkinsburg was just down the street and past the bridge from Point Breeze.

The neighborhood where Mother lived gave off quaint vibes. There was a series of connected brick homes with porches on a Cul Du Sac. Our home had a metal gate that I could not help but swing on when I was younger despite knowing it would get me in trouble. I cannot help but feel the sense of home when I think about the green carpet on the porch and the three little bushes in the yard along the house. Then there was the glider on the porch, of course. The kids, along with myself, would always break it from swinging on it. I had a few good friends in the area too. We were "the kids in the court."

I was excited to start a new chapter at Wilkinsburg. I heard stories about one of the elementary schools from a girl named Brazil that stayed in Penfield Court. She stayed a few houses up from Mother. Brazil lived in Wilkinsburg during the times she would stay with her father. She told me about her experiences in the area and stories about the friends she made. I ended up fitting right in when we moved onto Holland Avenue as anticipated.

Moving to Holland Avenue was a key period of transition for me. I was about to turn thirteen, and I was thrilled at the thought of becoming a teenager. When we moved to Wilkinsburg, I basically broke out of a shell. Still, I carried a sadness because there were things I was missing from the relationship with my mom. It seemed to be strained and awkward. She never taught me about boys, sex, or drugs. I was definitely unprepared for some of the situations I found myself in with the other kids in Wilkinsburg. I had to figure a lot of things out on my own. Family outings and quality time happened occasionally but were not expected or routine. I spent a lot of time out with my friends and learned from them and through experience.

From what I could see, my mom's struggle primarily involved men. She wanted to be in a relationship, and I remember her dating a couple of different guys when I was growing up, but it never worked out. She was often angry or unhappy, especially when it came to the relationship between her and my sister, Brielle's dad. My mom was hoping he would move into the house in Wilkinsburg with us, but he was not in the picture consistently like he should have been. He was unfaithful and made promises that he did not keep. I am sure this added to my mom's naturally angry disposition. She went to work, came home, and isolated herself from my sister and me. At times she would cook or bring fast food home. Other times, I would make something easy for my sister and me to eat. I was pretty mature and responsible at a young age, so I helped out a lot with Brielle in her father's absence, even picking her up occasionally from preschool at the Hosana House when I got out of school and walking us home safely. The dynamic was complicated, but I loved my sister's dad. To see how that relationship played out was hurtful and hard for me to understand at times. When he was around, things were nice; we looked like a family. Meanwhile, the relationship between my biological father and me changed once my sister, Autumn, was born. It was like he went from cherishing the ground I walked on to barely coming around. My dad's girlfriend never really cared for me because I was not her child.

Even though the relationship with my mom stayed stagnant, the first summer on Holland Avenue turned out to be amazing.

The neighborhood had plenty of kids. There was a mixture of apartment buildings, row homes, and single-family houses. We stayed in a brown and tan duplex apartment.

Being the new kid on the block meant I got a lot of attention. I was sized up by the girls to determine if I was friend worthy and the boys wanted to determine if I was pretty or not. Although people complimented my looks, like most girls, I was self-conscious, and my self-esteem wavered. I kept my wavy hair in a bun, and the boys would tease me about being a "thick" light-skinned girl. I initially could be found wearing baggy clothes when I got to Wilkinsburg, but as I gained confidence, I started to dress more feminine. When I started making the transition, the jealousy, hate, and betrayal that plagues teen girls started to come my way. Along with just about every new Jordan shoes that dropped, I was fitted in the designer brands like Roc a Wear and Pepe Jeans, to name a few. Some of the girls had a problem with that because they assumed, I was stuck up and conceited. Although I never really started trouble, trouble always seemed to find me. I did not like confrontation, but I was not one to back down from a fight either.

Being outside was how I met Jaren, my next-door neighbor. He lived in a big house with his mom, stepdad, and younger sisters. I was attracted to Jaren early on. He was tall with chestnut-colored skin and a wispy mustache that looked like it was trying to grow in. He resembled Lil Bow Wow, who all the girls thought was cute, that is until his personality began to show. Jaren would be no different. We would walk around, explore the neighborhood, meeting new kids as we went along. He was one of the first people to fill me in on what the block was like.

Jaren turned out to be my first boyfriend. He smiled and flirted with me constantly. We played outside together often, and one day we just started dating. I was taken by his looks and athletic ability. He played football for one of the neighborhood teams. To show support, I would take the bus to his games with some of the kids from the neighborhood and cheer him on. I stayed over at his house until late at night sometimes. Although we spent a lot of time together, neither of our parents really gave it much thought to a budding relationship between the two of us since he had sisters I would hang out with too. We would sneak around to kiss on his back porch. All the while, I was completely taken by his charm.

Jaren taught me my first lessons in love and relationships. These were hard lessons to learn indeed. He would flirt with some of the girls down the street and diss me in public. I ended up losing my virginity to him, which caused an even greater unhealthy bond that kept me around longer than I should have been. Things went too far one day when we went to Kennywood Amusement Park together. We wore matching outfits and everything, putting our relationship on full display. Still, he somehow ended up with another girl at the park, riding rides, sharing food, and being hugged up with her. He took pictures with her and really rubbed in the fact that he left me to be with this girl. I called my mom, crying for her to come get me. She was so furious that she forbade me from speaking to Jaren again. In true teenage fashion, however, I was outside talking to him the very next day. To my surprise, my mom came out and beat me with a plastic bat in front of everyone. I had welts everywhere. Ironically, I ended up at Jaren's house with his mom and stepfather consoling me and tending to my bruises.

Eventually, we broke up because he kept doing me wrong. I would cry often and felt weak. I thought I was turning into my mother, who I would see cry about my sister's dad. There I was, a young girl in a relationship being treated badly. I needed my mom during that time, and I could not talk to her. Seeing her struggle through relationships affected the way my first one turned out.

Fortunately, other people came into my life that I made genuine connections with while living in Wilkinsburg. One of which was Amir. Meeting Amir was a pivotal point in my life. We were introduced to each other by a friend I made named Diamond. She was one of the people I was introduced to early on as she lived right around the block. I met Diamond during one of the walks me and Jaren made to the store around the corner called Mike's. She and I would meet up at Mike's on a regular basis, Diamond became my first best friend. Asking our parents for change or saving up allowance meant we were going back and forth to the store, sometimes making multiple trips per day. Now and Laters, Cheetos, and soda were some of my favorites. It was during one of these trips to the store that I met Amir. It was easy to see why he was popular. Aside from his big personality, he was handsome, with nice hair, brown eyes, and caramel-colored skin. He was starting eighth grade, while I was starting seventh. Although he was what one would consider a pretty boy, he did not take shit from anybody.

He also spent a lot of time at Diamond's house, so I saw him often. He and I clicked right away. It was never a relationship type of vibe, but more so of an older brother and younger sister connection as we were just two years apart. At the time, he did not have any sisters, and although I had an older brother, we did not have a close relationship. I spent time hanging out at his house, where I got to know some of his family members, like Marvin, who went to a different school.

One of the hangout spots was on Amir's porch. His older brothers and friends would shoot dice and talk about girls. Amir knew a lot of people in the neighborhood since he grew up there. He would always have my back. During times when I had to fight, he never let anyone jump me. We later learned that we were related as cousins on my father's side of the family, yet and still, we remained sister and brother. Beyond the bond that formed with Amir, I formed one with his mom, Nita as well. Amir's mom filled the void left by mine. She told me about life, guys, and the streets. She looked out for me and provided some of the instructions I needed but did not get.

Every weekend was a new adventure, even as the school year settled in and fall began. Thinking back, we could have gotten into a lot of trouble. My mom did not know where I was, at times. Sometimes I would get home late at night or early in the morning, depending on how you view time. It was not unusual for me to come into the house at two in the morning. One of my favorite places to go was a 21 and under club called

"Jetz." Although there was a teen night in the hood, Jetz was just like any full-fledged adult bar, complete with a coat check. It was dark, and our clothes glowed under the black lights. People could sneak alcohol in, and the music was at full volume the entire night. There was a faint smell of marijuana smoke in the air at all times. We went to Jetz monthly while the other weekends were spent partying at someone's house. We were catching rides, borrowing cars, and taking buses, anything to get to the fun, even if that meant going to the next town.

Despite the fun I had outside of my house, the relationship with my mom seemed to get worse. I still had a difficult time communicating with her. Whenever I wanted to interact or tell her how my day was, her reaction was lined with irritation, as if I were a bother. *"Get to the point,"* she would say. I tried to tell her about my life, my friends, my dreams, but there was no room for meaningful dialogue. I needed guidance,

23

and I did not get it. As a result, I felt that neither one of us really knew each other. I always felt alone, so I looked at her differently. I did not always show her the utmost respect because our mother-daughter bond was not strong. I was lonely. Over time, I started staying out late. I started smoking and drinking, which resulted in physical confrontations with my mom. She would hit me when I talked back. I recall going to school, trying my best to hide bruises. I did not know how to process or explain how I felt without smart comments, eye-rolling, and lip-smacking.

Despite the problems I continued to have with my mom, one thing I definitely learned from her was a hard work ethic. I always admired and respected her hustle and independence. She kept a good job at various medical clinics in billing. She had associates at work, but the relationships were superficial. Nothing was long term with her. She also did part-time managing work for retail stores. She made sure we had a place to live, kept food in the house for us to eat, and most of what we wanted. My siblings and I were also fortunate that she did not drink and never used drugs.

When I needed to feel connected to someone, I would turn to Mother on Penfield Court. She was the one I had a maternal bond with. I remember she would always sleep in the living room by choice, so she was always there for me to talk to. She would play and watch cartoons with me. Mother helped me with my homework. I am like her in a lot of ways, one of which is a penchant for designer fashions. She also loved to read. I would meet Mother at her job downtown after I got out of school, and the two of us would spend the evening at Barnes and Noble or at the nearby jewelry store. Woodland Jewelers was my favorite. One of my favorites pieces she brought me was a Mickey Mouse charm with my name engraved on it along with matching earrings.

Character jewelry was a trend back then. All the girls could be seen wearing their favorite cartoon characters. Some of my fondest memories of Mother was when she would come home from work and drink a vermouth cocktail. It was always made with olives. I would beg for the marinating olives because I thought they made the drink look so cool. When she was in a good mood, she would let me have them. My grandmother was the one who taught me lessons about when to keep my mouth shut and the art of "keeping people out of your business." In the years to come, she provided me with love, support, and the advice I needed to be a strong woman.

Chapter 3

"Have you met Keisha yet?" Amir asked Ava as they met up in the hallway to go to the cafeteria.

"Mmmm... maybe. What does she look like?" Ava responded.

"She's in 8th grade with me. Tall, kinda big, and she got short hair," he added.

"I'm not really sure. I'd have to see her face," Ava said.

"Well, Imma introduce you to her. She's cool and is one of the most popular girls in school." Ava and Amir started down the lunch line, and as they made their way to a table, Amir glanced towards the doors and threw his left hand into the air. "Hey, Keisha!" he shouted, waving her over.

Ava looked up and saw a tall, brown skin girl coming their way. When Keisha made her way through the line like the others, she went over to Ava and Amir to sit down. Ava looked at the bigger girl sitting across from her and could not help but notice that she was not very pretty and her once white shirt was a bit dingy.

"Ava, this is Keisha..." Amir gestured, "...and Keisha, this my sister Ava," he continued.

Keisha glanced at Amir, then to Ava, and back to Amir. "That ain't ya sister," she said dubiously.

"Don't be a hater," Amir laughed.

"Whatever, Amir," Keisha rolled her eyes playfully. "Hey, boo, nice to meet you," Keisha smiled at Ava. The two asked each other questions about where they were from and who they knew around the neighborhood.

Keisha and Ava became friends fast. Although she was two years older than Ava, Keisha was used to hanging out with younger crowds. She was cool to hang out with. Everyone in the neighborhood knew her mom; Angie was out in the streets a lot. Angie would make too many trips to "talk" to the boys in the white t-shirts in front of the corner store for it to be just a coincidence. Her mom was obviously on something, no matter how much Keisha tried to deny it. Still, Keisha was popular because her house was the spot. Her mom would charge a dollar fee for neighborhood teens to come party in her basement on the weekends. They were allowed to do pretty much anything they wanted, unsupervised. If you hand an extra five dollars, Angie would even sell you a shot of whatever bottom shelf vodka she had on hand. Some of the most fun times were in that basement.

"What are you doing this weekend?" Keisha asked Ava, Amir, and Adonis at lunch early during the school week.

"Shit," Adonis responded first. "Why?" he continued.

"Cause my mom said I could have another party this weekend. It will be the first one since school started back," Keisha announced.

Amir rolled his eyes. "I'll go," Ava said.

She had only been to one of Keisha's parties over the summer, but she had a good time. There was a good mix of ages there, and a few people from other hoods would often slide through.

"If I come thru, I ain't staying long," Amir chimed in.

He was not really into house parties. He was so well known in the neighborhood that he sometimes got tired of seeing the same faces. Amir, along with Marvin and Adonis, mostly enjoyed going to other parts of town to party. Not only that, Keisha's basement got hot and funky too quickly, in his opinion. The bricks would sweat with the heat of bodies dancing and grinding for hours. The floor would be sticky with spilled soda and liquor. After a short while, people would start to stink. There were a few chairs and patched-up couches in the basement, a perfect place for a young, fresh couple of teens to make out and play touchy-feely. He might find a girl there he had not seen yet, so he agreed to make sure he stopped by before Keisha started to make a fuss.

***

Ava stumbled over a black bookbag that sat in the middle of the aisle in English class. Sincere "Sin" Collins was asleep in class again and had not bothered to make sure his bag was out of the way before putting his head down.

"Damn Sin! You gone kill somebody!" Ava shouted, nearly dropping her books.

"My bad. You straight?" Sin looked up groggily.

He had marks on his forehead from the folds on the sleeves of his Enyce jacket being pressed up against his face for so long. He moved his bag under his seat and put his head back down. Ava thought Sin was handsome. He was light skin with a slim build and brown eyes. Too bad, he was not her type. Sin never did his class assignments or participated during group discussions, but somehow, he did remarkably on his quizzes and tests.

Ava had two classes with Sin, and they, along with a school bus full of other students, went to Forbes vocational school together for half days. Despite this, they did not speak much. Sin went to culinary arts classes while Ava went for the cosmetology program. A bus transported the group from Wilkinsburg to the vocational school each morning.

Ava stood outside the school, rubbing her shoulders vigorously to keep warm. She was waiting for the Forbes bus at the designated pick-up spot. It was fall, and the air was always cooler in the mornings than later in the day. Sin glanced over to Ava as she stood quietly but clearly uncomfortable. He moved behind her slyly and took off his jacket to slide it around her. Ava smiled reflexively as she realized what Sin was doing. She had not seen him make the move.

"Oooh. Thanks!" she said gratefully as she quickly slipped her hands in the pockets. She could still feel the warmth of his body heat. Ava felt both flattered and relieved.

"Can I sit next to you? I don't want you tryna run off with my jacket," Sin joked as they boarded the bus.

With a smile, Ava agreed and slid over to make room for him. From then on, they always sat together in the back of the bus, where they made out, touched each other, and exchanged hickeys. They shared kisses and cracked jokes, soon becoming quite an affectionate couple. It was nothing short of a special relationship.

Ava could tell Sin came from a good background. He was a gentleman, which made him completely different from Jaren. Sin had a lot of respect for women, likely from seeing his parents in a healthy relationship. Not only that, he was also an amazing cook. People would ask him for food all the time on the way back from Forbes.

"Aye, man, I know you cooked something up in class. What you got?" Jessica asked, with her nose pointing in the air to take in the aroma. Jessica was always one of the first people to come running to the back of the bus to see what meals Sin had in the container he brought from class each day.

"Fam, that smells bomb as hell," Jessica added as she started to lean forward over the school bus seat.

"Hold on, Jessica," Sin replied and turned to Ava. "Hey, baby, you want some of this?" Sin always made sure he offered Ava his delicious creations before anyone else. Ava felt cherished.

"What is it?" she asked.

"It's a pot pie," he replied. Ava politely declined as she was not particularly hungry.

35

"Girl, you crazy," Jessica said, nearly grabbing the container from Sin's hands.

"Damn! Move ya greedy ass back. Imma give you some." Sin maneuvered the container further away from Jessica.

Sin and Ava talked on the phone daily. Eventually, he started going with Ava to Keisha's, well Angie's, basement parties mostly to duck off and make out. In the following weeks, Sin and Ava spent a lot of time at Keisha's house in the basement during the weekdays when no parties were going on. Keisha agreed to let the two love birds come to her house to be together. They smoked and drank down there during times they could get their hands on a bottle.

When they were not at Keisha's house, Sin and Ava would go to Mother's hose. Patrice, Ava, and Brielle had been living back with Mother while Patrice was in search of a new place for them to live after moving from

Holland Ave. With her mom's room being set up down in the basement meant it was quiet and secluded. Vonte was the only person there during the day, and he could not hear what was happening.

"You sure ya, mom ain't coming home?" Sin questioned nervously.

"No, she is at work. She'll be home around 5:30," Ava said reassuringly as the two slipped inside the house and down the stairs that lead to the basement.

They had plenty of time until Ava's mom arrived. Ava sat down on the twin-sized beds that were pushed together to make one and patted the space next to her, motioning for him to sit. Sin quickly forgot about his initial fears as he went over to sit next to her. After their usual kissing and touching, they decided to take it a step further. That Fall afternoon, Ava took Sin's virginity. A fact that was completely unknown to her at that point.

***

"You look gorgeous," Sin said as he took Ava's brown fur coat.

He took a step back to get a good look at her. Her long hair was in bouncy spiral curls that cascaded down her back. She wore a red, black, and silver Roc A Wear outfit that matched her new Air Jordan's. It was Christmas, and Ava had been invited to Sin's house. She was nervous, but luckily, she was not alone. One of her cousins was dating one of his best friends who was also at the dinner, so she felt a little more at ease. After meeting and mingling with his family for a couple of hours, the two couples ventured off into the neighborhood. Ava, Sin, Crystal, and Ray were dressed in their Christmas attire, looking for a place to smoke.

Christmas was just one of the holidays they spent together.

***

The clock read 10:30 am. Ava sat anxiously in third period. It was February 14th. Each Valentine's day, the science club sold carnations and donated the proceeds to the American Heart Association. Every girl in the school knew the club members disbursed the carnations around this time.

Finally, after what seemed like an eternity, the door finally opened, and two students wearing red t-shirts with the school science club logo stepped inside. They were holding handfuls of carnations as they started calling out names. "Jasmine... Brittany... Shanice...Ava..." Ava squealed in excitement as she made her way to the front to gather a half dozen roses.

She read the sheet of paper attached to the bundle with a ribbon. "Ava, Happy Valentine's Day baby. Love Sin." Her face reddened as she took in the sweet scent of the beautiful mix of pink and red roses. At lunchtime, Ava ran to Sin, carnations in hand, to give him a kiss.

"Thank you for the flowers, babe," she said.

"Come with me," Sin responded with a smile as he took her hand in his and led her out of the cafeteria.

"Where are we going?" Ava asked.

"It's a surprise, just come on," he reassured.

The two walked towards the front entrance of the school. "Wait here," he instructed.

Sin quickly disappeared behind a corner leading to the front of the building. When he came back around, he was holding what looked like a giant flowerpot with a big teddy bear inside. There were balloons coming from all sides that read, "I Love You." She just could not believe it. Sin's father dropped off the gift midday. Ava's eyes started to tear as she cupped her mouth in surprise. There were a few jealous faces when she returned to the cafeteria with her gift. Sin was in love with Ava, and it showed.

***

The winter weather started to turn warmer as spring set in. Just like the snow started to fade away, so did Sin and Ava's relationship. She could feel that they would probably be breaking up soon. They began to argue over petty things, which was aggravating to both of them. Still, being teenagers meant they were not able to resolve conflicts between each other very well. They even started to sit in different seats on the Forbes bus. One day, on the way back to school, Ava leaned forward to speak to Sin, who sat diagonally from her on one of the bus seats.

"Hey. Can I have the picture we took during Christmas? I really need it for my photo collage," Ava asked flatly.

"Which ones?" Sin asked. There were several photos taken that night. Mostly of him and Ava, but there was one she took solo.

"Just the one of me," Ava replied, shrugging her shoulders. She could tell that this angered him immediately.

"Oh, you don't want any of the ones with both of us?" he questioned.

Ava raised an eyebrow and shrugged her shoulders. "No," she replied, smacking her lips.

Sin snapped. "Boyz, I ain't giving you shit!"

Ava grew furious just as quickly. "Stop being a lame and just give me the fuckin picture!" she demanded.

The two went back and forth until they both stood up, intending to get in each other's faces. "Whoa! Hold on, ya'll ain't bout to be fighting," Jessica said as she rose to stand in the middle of the confrontation.

She was tall and thick. Still, she would not be able to break up a fight between the two if it came down to it. "Jessica, you need to move out the way!" Ava said.

Jessica threw her long arms up in an effort to maintain the distance between the feuding pair. Ava and Sin continued to hurl insults at each other. Realizing that she could not take a swing at Sin without hitting Jessica, Ava took the still sticky blow pop she had in her mouth moments before and threw it at Sin.

"You crazy bitch!" Sin yelled as the sucker bounced off his shirt, leaving a sticky stain.

"Ooooooh." The other students on the bus grew quiet as the argument continued to intensify.

"I got ya bitch," Ava yelled as she spit right in Sin's face, smack dead in the middle of his forehead.

When the students got back from Forbes, word of the bus incident spread through the school like wildfire. Sin's older sister found out and met up with Ava after the final bell rang to fight. His sister walked up to Ava pounding her fist in her hands as she drew near. As the two started to argue, a crowd grew around them. Out of nowhere, Ava felt the stinging pain and heard the audible thud as a fist made contact with the side of her face. Her custom Mickey Mouse earring flew from her earlobe with the force of the strike.

Pain set in immediately, and the side of her face reddened.

While she was not severely injured by the blow, it caused a shock to her system as it caught her completely off guard. Sin had run up to Ava while she was arguing with his sister and punched her in the face. He didn't stop, running right through the crowd that formed. There were several gasps that came from onlookers as they witnessed the teenage boy hit his ex-girlfriend in the face. They were so in love just a couple of weeks ago. The arguing between Ava and Sin's sister came to a halt as it just seemed strange to fight at that point. The crowd quickly broke up once it was clear that nothing else of interest was going to happen.

Ava immediately thought to call Amir. She explained the important details of the altercation on the bus and about the punch in the face.

"I'll fight him," Amir said simply. "But you know we all live in the same hood, so it's gone cause big problems," he warned.

She decided against having Amir retaliate. Later that night, she and her mother considered whether or not to press charges against Sin. They would have no problem making a case against him, seeing as how he hit her in front of a crowd of middle and high school students. Though her face was not swollen too much, it was sore. It was the insult more than the injury that left Ava fuming. After a few cold compresses, to make sure any swelling was kept at a minimum, Ava began to cool off and think. "*I did spit in his face. He was outta pocket for hitting me though. Could he press charges against me for spittin' on him*?"

When Ava woke up the next day, she decided that she would be the bigger person and apologize to Sin for spitting on him. She had never done anything like that before, but somehow, he just made her that mad. Still, if she did get Amir to fight him, people in the neighborhood would take sides, likely starting an ongoing feud. If she pressed charges, it could jeopardize his vocational school training. Ava knew Sin had real talent in the kitchen, and she did not want to take things that far. The two boarded the bus the next day as if nothing happened. They were not speaking but sat near the back of the bus as always. Ava leaned into the aisle and got Sin's attention from a couple of seats up. She motioned for him to come nearer. Sin leaned into her from an adjacent empty seat.

"I just wanted to say that I love you, and I'm sorry," Ava said genuinely.

"I'm sorry too, and I love you, Ava," Sin echoed.

The two smiled in unison. Although they were on speaking terms, after that, the relationship between the two was not the same. They were civil, but there was no reconciling the once beautiful teenage love.

Chapter 4

Ava tapped her long, glittery pink nails on her desk as she looked up at the clock waiting for geometry class to start. The seats were filling quickly, but a couple of the ones around her were still empty. As she noted the time, a short girl with a crispy wrap walked into the classroom slowly. A few other eyes glanced to the doorway as they quickly realized that she was a new student.

"Come sit next to me," Ava called out to the girl from near an open window. "Sit here. Before Dante does," she gestured towards the seat next to her. "He told me first period that he was in this class. He always be tryna talk to me, he's so annoying," said Ava.

"Okay," the new girl replied as she sat, glad that someone was being friendly to her. "I'm Remy," she said.

Remy was short, about 5'1, thin with caramel-colored skin. "I'm Ava. You weren't here last year," she noted.

"No, I just moved here from Hazelwood," Remy replied.

"Where do you live?" Ava continued.

"I live two blocks away on the same street as the school," Remy answered.

"That must be nice, especially when it's cold outside. You can wait for me after school then, and we can walk home together. Let me see your schedule."

Remy held out her small hand. Her nails were fly too. They were royal blue with white and silver line designs. The tips had carefully placed rhinestones on them. Ava asked where Remy she got them done. Remy's eyes lit up as she talked about her favorite nail shop.

"You have to go on Wednesdays because that is free design day," she informed Ava.

The two talked briefly but with genuine interest before the bell rang to start class. A sisterhood that would stand the test of time was formed that day, in that very moment.

Ava introduced Remy to Amir right after geometry class. Being at a new school could be awkward, so Ava decided to make it a little easier for Remy to get to know people. After class, they went into the hallway and waited for him near his locker. When Amir approached, he looked curiously at Remy.

"Amir, this is Remy; she's new. Remy, this is my brother Amir." Remy smiled at him nervously. She thought he was fine.

"When you get here?" he asked, making conversation so he could look directly into her eyes for a few moments more.

"We moved here like four days ago," Remy replied, staring right back into his eyes.

The two instantly liked each other, and it did not take long for them to start dating. From then on, Remy, Amir, and Ava were nearly inseparable. Ava introduced Remy to Keisha and a few other girls they ran into during and after class. The fact that the two of them became best friends so quickly drew the attention of some of the other girls Ava made friends with at school and home.

"Damn, she acts like she doesn't know us no more." A couple of Ava's friends said half-jokingly. Not everyone liked Remy. She was little with a big personality. The fact that Amir never took his eyes off her had a few girls jealous too. Remy was not one to back down from a fight, though, and Ava always had her back.

Ava, Remy, Adonis, and Amir sat at the table at Angelos Pizza discussing the fight that broke out at Jetz the weekend before. Every Friday and Saturday night, the hole in the wall pizza joint was packed full of teenagers. The music was often louder than necessary as they all took turns being the DJ and playing with the jukebox. Despite the place having roaches, the food was delicious and a popular hangout spot. The four of them just had a smoke session on Remy's porch, and the munchies were setting in quickly. Ava was on her second slice of her Sicilian pizza when Keisha and Tonya walked in towards the counter. On the way to order, Keisha walked past the group.

"Hey Keisha," Amir said first.

"Hey," she responded. Looking Ava right in the face, she said, "Damn, I ain't get invited to ya'll little pizza night, I see."

"Umm, we were all chillin at Remy's house and kinda just decided to walk down here," Ava responded.

She started to feel bad that she was leaving Keisha out more and more. Ava just had more in common with Remy and had not paid attention to how little she was hanging out with the other girls she met when she first came.

"Yeah, whatever," Keisha said as she continued to walk past, side-eyeing Remy. "*Fake ass*," Keisha thought to herself.

"Cuh, homies, that bitch trippin, she better go ahead," Remy said, giving Keisha the same look, she had given her. "Did ya'll see how she looked at me?" she continued.

"Ya'll girls are a mess," Adonis said as he took another bite of pizza, not at all concerned about what he saw as petty girl drama.

She looked towards the counter at Keisha. She was wearing the light blue fitted shirt Ava's mother bought for her a couple of months ago. Since her mom worked as a manager for K-Mart part-time as a side hustle, she was often combing through the clearance racks for clothes. Occasionally she would buy items for Keisha since she knew Angie had other priorities for her money.

"She ain't have to look at me all crazy n shit though," Remy replied.

Later that night, Ava sent Keisha a text trying to spark a light conversation. To her surprise, Keisha never responded. "*I got too much other shit to worry about.*" Ava thought as she looked at her text messages a few hours later. "*She will come back around.*"

Despite the uncertainty of Keisha and Ava's friendship, Ava had no problems making other friends. Word was going around that a group of older girls in the neighborhood had formed a little clique of about ten girls or so and had even given themselves a name. It was not at all like a gang, just a tight-knit group that went to the movies and parties together. Sometimes they even dressed alike. This gave Ava and some of her friends the idea to form their own clique they called the DAB Squad. It consisted of girls around the neighborhood that was about the same age and fell in together naturally. Some of them were close to Amir's family.

Generally, the girls would find the parties, go to the mall together, and sometimes they even got up on Sunday mornings and took the bus to church together. Ava thought it would be fun, although a couple of the girls looked at the group as a built-in backup for anytime a fight broke out. One of which was a girl named Raquel, a.k.a. Rocky. She was one of the biggest troublemakers in Wilkinsburg, always fighting, starting rumors, and getting arrested.

One day after school, Rocky was outside, causing a commotion about who she was going to fight next. She was walking with her sidekick, Candy. At the sound of drama, other girls started gathering around; no one wanted to miss at least seeing a fight if not participating in one. Rocky announced that she was heading towards Homewood to fight a girl she had beef with. Candy ended up calling Remy to come join, and although Ava wanted no parts, she decided to go only with the intention of looking out for her best friend. If Wilkinsburg was amassing a group to go fight, she knew the Homewood girls would be doing the same.

As the girls got closer to the border of Wilkinsburg and Homewood, Rocky called the girl she intended to fight, asking where she was.

"I see y'all. Ya'll ain't deep," the voice on the other line said.

Apparently, the girl could see them, but Rocky was unable to locate her. She must have been in one of the houses. Rocky looked around to the fifteen girls that stood around with her feeling confident. She continued to argue with the girl on the phone. As the group of Wilkinsburg girls drew closer to the border, the unexpected happened. A pickup truck full of girls pulled up, along with a few other cars, also filled with girls, about thirty in all. It was clear that the Homewood girls outnumbered the Wilkinsburg girls about 2 to 1. Ava was torn. She had family in Homewood. Rocky and the other girl started to fight, which quickly turned into an all-out brawl. People were running around, punching each other randomly. It was a chaotic scene as people were yelling and hitting faces; they never laid eyes on before that moment. Eventually, it came to a head when one girl started screaming in agony.

"She got stabbed!" someone yelled.

This caught everyone's attention. Ava ran over to check on the girl. There was blood dripping everywhere, and although she could not immediately tell where the blood was coming from, it was clear by the sheer volume that she was injured badly and would likely need stitches.

"Lets go! This shit is outta hand!" Ava grabbed Remy, and the two started running back towards Wilkinsburg.

The rest of the crowd started to disburse once it was revealed that someone had a weapon. At that point, no one knew who had the knife. As the girls ran off while the victim still laid in the street, screaming in pain. The squad did not last long after that.

Ava and Remy decided to make their own fun after the neighborhood brawl. Being in a group so large meant taking on other people's problems. This put a further strain on Ava's relationships with the other Wilkinsburg girls, but she did not care. At this point, Ava was working and focusing on school more than worrying about who thought she was acting differently.

***

"Guess what I got," Remy said excitedly as she bounced on the edge of Ava's bed on a Thursday evening after school.

"What?" Ava said curiously, moving towards Remy's oversized Louis Vuitton backpack.

Both Remy and Ava got matching bags during one of their trips to New York. Remy pulled out a camcorder and a couple of blank tapes.

"We are going to take this to the party tomorrow," Remy announced.

"Where did you get that from?" Ava looked on with interest.

"It's daddy's," Remy replied.

The pair decided to go to Penn Hills for a sweet sixteen party for one of the town's most popular girls. The night of the party Ava and Remy recorded everything; the dancing, the smoking, and even a fight that broke out. In the coming weeks, they took the recorder everywhere with them. It was like their own version of video diaries or a vlog. People would jump right in front of the camera to say something silly or show off their outfits when they saw Ava and Remy recording.

It was a Saturday night, a.k.a. "Devil's Night," in Wilkinsburg, right before the weather started turning cold. It was one of the last chances for the Wilkinsburg teens to have fun in the streets before they were dusted with frost and snow. Ava and Remy sat on the porch at Amir's house with a few of his friends when they saw a couple of girls they knew walk up with a few cartons of eggs.

"What y'all bout to cook with all them eggs?" Ava asked.

"We ain't cooking shit. Bout to throw them at Tasha's punk ass house," one of the girls replied.

"Why?" asked one of the boys who also sat on Amir's porch.

"Cause she was talking shit, and now she won't come out the house, so when the sun goes down, we bout to egg her shit," another girl replied with a grin.

Ava looked at Remy. The two had never egged a house, but it sounded like an event well-suited to be tapped with the camcorder. "Let's go get some eggs," Ava said mischievously as she thought of whose house she wanted to hit.

"Hell yeah," Remy agreed as the two started to make their way to Rim's corner store for a few cartons.

Ava considered going to her house to get some but thought better of it. Her mom would be pissed if she knew Ava took food out of the house to play with. Plus, if she went into the house, Patrice just might make her stay in for the night.

That night, about a dozen houses ended up with eggs stuck to windows along with stained stairs and doors. Word got around that there would be a mass egging, so the streets ended up filled with teens ducking, dodging, and throwing eggs both at houses and each other. Ava and Remy took turns throwing and recording. Seeing how much fun the girls were having. The guys decided to join in, but by the time they made the decision, there were no eggs left at the store. The next best thing was to use paintballs as far as they were concerned.

"Pop, pop, pop!" The air gun of the paintball sounded as the guys drove past and shot pellets at the girls who were on foot running, ducking, and dodging while still throwing eggs: one hit, Ava in the leg.

"What the fuck!" she yelled, looking down at the green paint that splatted her jeans.

Even though it was a paintball, the impact still hurt. Candy was hit in the back of the head with a yellow paintball. It splattered everywhere as she screamed out in both surprise and pain. "They got a paintball gun," someone yelled. Recorder in hand, Remy ran around the neighborhood videotaping who was getting shot with the paintball gun. The reaction the other kids had to being hit and seeing the paint stain their clothes was priceless. As the egg fight turned into a paintball fight, the boys had an unfair advantage. None of the girls owned a paintball gun. The fun came to an end when all sides ran out of ammo. As the morning dawned, all could see that the neighborhood looked like a disaster zone, the sunlight revealing what occurred the night before.

There was paint splatter where the boys failed to hit their targets. There were eggshells, toilet paper, and even some fruits and vegetables lining the street and sidewalks. Apparently, people started throwing anything once they ran out of eggs. It was truly a night to remember, especially because Ava and Remy caught it all on tape.

Chapter 5

Over the years, I was learning that young love comes and goes. I started dating Wauseem Williams, around the spring of eleventh grade, almost immediately after Sin and I broke up. Wauseem was easy on the eyes. He had a caramel complexion and the kind of long hair a girl could not help but want to run her fingers through. He was fitted and had infinite swag. Not only was he handsome, but he was also the varsity quarterback. Students and teachers alike enjoyed seeing him on the field. He was smart, maintaining a 3.6 GPA while playing sports. The real bonus was that Wauseem had a younger brother named Malachi. Both were a similar shade of caramel with a handsome smile. The school could not get enough of the Williams brothers. This made Wauseem a girl magnet. He liked to flirt and did not really care much for their feelings.

Wauseem was in my history class with Mr. Barnes. He sat in front of me and would turn around to talk and crack jokes. "What's up, Ava. What did you do this weekend?" he would ask, flashing his priceless grin. My stomach would do flips when he smiled, but I would never tell him that. One day, he invited me to his house after school, and I went over to hang out with him. I was cool with the idea because my friend Isla was already dating his brother Malachi.

One invitation turned into two, which turned into three, until I found myself hanging out with him, Isla, and his brother several nights a week. I ended up getting Isla a job at Wendy's, and after our shifts, we would take food to the Williams brothers and chill at their house. Isla was light-skin, pretty with green eyes. It made sense to me that she and Malachi were attracted to each other, but when it came to Wauseem and me, I was like, "What am I doing?" Knowing that he ran through girls made me think I would only be used. Still, I could not help but be attracted to him.

Despite my reservations, Wauseem and I became closer the more we spent time together, but sadly, just as quickly as our relationship started, it came to an end. When summer came around, his dad moved him and his brother to West Virginia to stay with their uncle for a better education. Still, we kept talking during the summer. One Saturday morning, he called me right before he was about to leave. I could hear the sadness in his voice.

"I'm about to go now, Ava. I'm going to miss you," he said. "I love you," he continued.

"I love you too," I said without thinking twice.

"We're going to stay together, okay?" Wauseem said, half asking and half making a statement. He and I kept in contact over the years, which led to some relationship issues down the road.

***

It was the fall of our senior year. The days were still warm, but the nights were growing colder. The changing seasons meant that homecoming was drawing near. The school's football players, one of which was Sin, practiced daily after classes let out. Homecoming was the highlight of the fall semester, and I decided that I wanted to run for court. Ever since I was a little girl, I imagined myself being crowned queen. I was actively working on my self-esteem issues, but I did not let self-doubt stop me from trying to earn the crown. Besides, I was meant to sparkle. I always kept up a vaunt appearance, with the latest shoes, colorful hairstyles, and of course, jewelry. It was only right for me to shine. So, when the time came around, I just wanted to take a chance.

I contacted my aunt Nicky from Leechburg, about an hour away, for her assistance. She was what you would consider a girly-girl, very crafty and creative. When I told her I was running for homecoming court, she went into planning and crafting mode with the utmost excitement. Aunt Nicky made posters for me while insisting that we make business cards saying, "Vote for Ava" to attach to the goods I would be handing out. She really ran with the project, which was a huge help to me. I was more than thrilled with her effort. She believed in me. My mom was excited too, and helped a great deal with my campaign. The students running for court campaigned for about a week, and I had something available for my fellow students for every day of the week, including candy bags, cupcakes, juice, and chips.

As one can imagine, running for homecoming queen can get competitive, even downright nasty. It brought out the worst in some of my classmates. One of the girls I ran against, Vanessa also liked Sin, but they never got together. When I started dating him, she made a point to continue to be all in his face, flirting as often as possible. Not only that, Vanessa's cousin and I got into a fight when I lived on Holland Avenue. It was like the two of us were destined to be rivals. Besides Vanessa, there were girls that ran for homecoming court who had grown up in Wilkinsburg, having gone to both elementary and middle school there. Yet, here I was, rising in popularity and gaining the favor of the student body. The hate came to an ugly head when the words "*Fat Bitch*" was written on one of the posters my aunt made, right across my face. The incident was addressed, but we never found out who did it officially.

Despite the jealous actions of my peers, I remained positive as long as I could. It was not until the day the votes were counted that I began to doubt that I would win. One of Vanessa's friends stole the garbage bag with discarded votes that had been counted. When they got home, they counted the ballots and determined that Vanessa had won. At least that was the rumor going around school the next day. At that point, I started to cope with the realization that I lost.

The following day was the announcement for homecoming court. Students, teachers, and parents poured into the concrete stands surrounding Graham-Field to watch the game. There was excitement in the air as the crowd anxiously waited for the results at half time. My heart was racing, and I was all nerves by the time the first half of the game ended. The sun was bright, and I began to sweat from the heat and pressure. Finally, one of the teachers on the homecoming committee grabbed a microphone and walked towards the center of the field. The candidates were escorted to the center thereafter. "It is the moment you all have been waiting for. Time to announce this year's homecoming court." The loud murmuring of the crowd began to die down as the teacher continued speaking. "I will start with the freshmen class first..." I made eye contact with Vanessa, who had a smug grin on her face.

One by one, I heard names being called, starting with the underclassmen. It seemed to take forever to get to the seniors. There was a pause for cheering and clapping as each person was named. The next thing I heard was my mom yelling, "Oh my God, she won!" from the bleachers. After the announcer was done, I was the last one standing.

I cannot fully describe the feelings of shock and amazement I felt at that moment. It was surreal. Despite my insecurities with myself, I felt that I accomplished something significant. For the first time as a teenager, I felt my mom, and I connected. We bonded during my campaign. Not only that, I won the support of my peers and could not wait to celebrate. Oddly enough, Keisha crowned me. She won homecoming queen the year before, and the tradition was for the previous queen to crown the winner thereafter. At that point, we were not really speaking. Our friendship faded out as I hung out with Remy more, and the two of them did not get along. She said congratulations, but we were short with each other. At that moment, I thought little of what our friendship turned into, but in the future, things between us would grow even more uncomfortable. Nevertheless, the game continued, and everyone was ready for the dance later that night.

The homecoming dance was fun, even though I was slightly upset that Wauseem was not able to come with me. I knew that it was a longshot for his dad to allow him to come back up from West Virginia after just moving a couple of months prior. Not long after homecoming, Wauseem and I had the familiar, *"She reminds me of you"* conversation. You know, the one where the guy tells the girl from long distance that he is talking to someone else that reminds him of her. As if that makes things any better. Still, the friends I did go out with had fun, and we took lots of pictures. I opted out of the traditional dress in favor of a black and gold, velour, and sheer Roc-A-Wear outfit. It was a capri suit with sheer crowns and cherries on it. The look was complimented by a waterfall cascade hairstyle and gold heels. The previous day I got my nails done at Queen's on Penn Avenue. My favorite nail artist was a Vietnamese man who very humorously referred to us as the "CHOWS" or "Chicken Heads of Wilkinsburg." All things said, no one could tell me I was not fly, but we did not stay long. My friends and I wanted to drink and smoke, and we knew that wasn't about to go down with school staff around. I did not even dance because it required the confidence that I still lacked at that point. I was just ready to go to the after-party. Isla had her mom's van for the entire night, so we were able to fit a bunch of people inside to go to the rooms we booked.

The motel we went to was a cash only establishment, the Sunrise Inn, located in Monroeville. Although I was quite certain it had bed bugs, it was affordable for teenagers, and the staff looked the other way when it came to marijuana smoke. Amir and Remy met us out there, as the two did not go to the game or the dance. The rest of the night was spent smoking, drinking, and running from room to room. The music played loudly, and we had a good time replaying the homecoming announcement for everyone to see.

"I knew you were going to win, Ava. Congratulations, sis," Amir said as he took a sip from his cup.

"Thanks. I didn't think I would," I responded.

"I told people I would beat they ass if they didn't vote for you," Amir joked.

"I knew it!" Ava played along. "But seriously, thank you for the support," I added. Moments like this were common for Amir and me. We were each other's biggest supporters.

***

The weather was getting colder as Thanksgiving approached. I still had good energy from winning homecoming queen as I had made even more friends after that. Not only that, my mom purchased a three-bedroom house in Penn Hills for us. Classes were going well, that is until I got kicked out of Wilkinsburg High School. It was over something stupid, of course. I regret what occurred, but it all happened so fast. A girl named Amber sat behind me in English class. She went to Forbes and rode the bus with Sin and me the previous year. She was cool but always goofy with boys. She tried too hard to get attention, which was exactly the problem that day.

Amber sat directly behind me, and the boy she liked sat directly in front of me. I patiently sat in the middle of the two, as they exchanged love taps from time to time. During the middle of a lesson, while we were all trying to learn, my patience began to run thin. Amber decided to play around with the boy in front of me even though he clearly wanted nothing to do with her that day. She started reaching around me to touch him and talked loudly behind my ear. Still, he paid her little mind. Finally, my frustration at being distracted made me snap.

I turned around and said, "He just doesn't like you! Could you be quiet so we can learn? He doesn't like you! He is not giving you any attention!"

The class was dead silent until someone started to laugh and crack jokes at her expense. I am certain she was thoroughly embarrassed because she snapped back at me immediately. We started arguing until we eventually stood up. She decided to make a smart remark, "Oh yeah! Well... that's why you used to give Sin head on the back of the bus!" I gasped because she told a blatant lie; I had done no such thing. In an effort to cool down, I got up to walk towards the door. My intention was to take a walk in the hallway. Things escalated, however, when Amber would not stop talking. I picked up a tape dispenser from the teacher's desk as I passed it and threw it at her.

Before the altercation went any further, security guards came and escorted us out of the classroom. Amber and I were taken to the principal's office. I had been there often because we were related through Amir. I would stop to say hello on my own or involuntarily when I was in trouble. Whenever I did something that required adult notification, I called Amir's mom instead of my own. As a senior, his office was a place that I was quite familiar with. This particular trip was different because security was grossly negligent in putting Amber and I both in the office together... alone. When the door closed and the two of us found ourselves just inches away from each other, I took a swing. The entire office staff could see the fight through the glass windows of the principal's office. When the principal came in, he gave me an "*I can't save you now*" look. I had to call my mom to explain what I had done.

I was suspended for three days and was potentially facing expulsion. I was nervous the entire time because I was a senior. I did not want to get kicked out during my last year; I had just won homecoming queen after all. When I finally went back to school, I was told I would be suspended for an additional seven days. Apparently, they were not ready to have me back in class yet. My mom refused the extended suspension and informed the school that I would not be returning. As soon as we left Wilkinsburg High, we drove directly to Taylor Allderdice High School for enrollment. It would have been my assigned high school if I still lived at Mother's House. I knew some students that went there, but still, I was upset because I wanted to graduate from Wilkinsburg. I was hurt about the forced transition for quite a while.

Chapter 6

Ava fit in easily at Taylor Allderdice High School. She knew a lot of students there from Mother's neighborhood. Still, there were many new faces, like Yves. Ava was not interested in Yves when they first met. He was cute enough, with light skin and dark hair. Still, he did not invest much time into his appearance like Ava was used to. He would wear the same blue jeans with a green stain on the back pocket a couple of days in a row. "*How strange*," she thought. "*Didn't he wear those yesterday? Why wouldn't he change*?" Yves, on the other hand, fell in love with Ava instantly.

The two had three classes together. During their senior project class, Yves initially sat next to a girl named Shantell, with who he flirted with openly. When Ava caught his attention, he started sitting behind her. He would lean in close to whisper in her ear.

Oddly enough, one day, he even licked her lobe.

"Ewww! What the hell?" Ava said reflexively, wiping her ear.

Yves grinned wildly. Still, she eventually exchanged numbers with him. He was attentive, always looking for her in the hallways between classes. One night he heard her coughing and clearing her throat on the phone, so the next day, he found her before first period to give her a pack of cough drops. Yves lived in Penn Hills too. Before long, they started riding the city bus to school together.

Although Ava was getting to know Yves, she still spoke to Wauseem in West Virginia from time to time. Wauseem stayed in contact with several people from the Wilkinsburg area, including a girl named Sasha, who also went to Taylor Allderdice High School and knew Yves. Once Sasha made the connection that Ava was talking to them both, she eagerly brought the information to Yves, who simply could not handle the thought of Ava being involved with someone else, whether they were just friends or not.

"I'm done with you!" Yves stated firmly in the hallway one morning at school when he saw Ava. "I know all about Wauseem. Sasha told me. She said you are never gone stop messin' wit that dude!" he continued.

Ava gulped. She was caught completely off guard. Ava could tell by his clenched fists and red face that he was serious. When he was done speaking his piece, he turned and walked off down the corridor.

"Wait! Let me tell you..." Ava began after him, but he would not stop.

She felt it was best to give him a moment to calm down. When class was over, Ava went to go find him. "Yves." Ava walked up to him as he was coming out of Ms. Patterson's class. He started to move past her when she held up her hands.

"Just stop. Let me talk to you," she said, pulling him off to the side. "I'm sorry. There is nothing going on between Wauseem and me. We are just friends, and besides, he lives in West Virginia now. We are not together."

Yves looked up to make eye contact with Ava. He had been looking towards the ground, kicking at a pen cap on the floor. Ava could see that he was starting to come around as the anger in his face softened. She continued. "I want to be with you, Yves." She said, looking directly into his eyes. He could not help but smile at Ava's last statement. The date was March 8th, 2007, and from that day forward, Yves and Ava were together. He would ride his bike and walk to her house, which was a considerable distance without a car; he was crazy about her.

Yves was sweet but had an ever-present anger problem. He would still talk and flirt with girls at school despite the scene he made when it came to Ava talking to Wauseem. In turn, she continued to speak to her former boyfriend in West Virginia. This sort of tit for tat caused a lot of problems that led to a lot of arguments not only in high school but years into the future.

***

Ava's difficulties soon extended beyond just Yves, eventually spilling into work. One day she went into Wendy's for her scheduled shift when Mrs. Marlaina, the manager, called her into the office.

"I need to talk to you," Mrs. Marlaina said as she motioned for Ava to sit in one of the chairs in the narrow office.

Ava looked around the walls lined with employee schedules and customer reviews.

Mrs. Marlaina sat down on the opposite side of a metal desk and sighed loudly. "I hate that this has even come up, Ava, but it has been brought to my attention that you stole Heather's check." Heather was an individual with special needs. She cleaned tables a few hours a week as part of a work program. Stealing from her was unconscionable and something that never once crossed Ava's mind.

"What! Are you serious right now?" Ava protested as her eyes began to fill with tears.

It was shocking that she was being accused of doing something like that. "You know I wouldn't steal from that lady!" Ava continued.

"I know, I know." Mrs. Marlaina waved her hands, motioning for Ava to calm down. "Isla told us that you stole the check. We are not going to fire you, but we do need to start an investigation because if you did not take it,

87

then someone else did," Mrs. Marlaina explained.

"Well, it had to be Isla because why else would she blame me for this. Where is this supposed check? How would I even cash it?" Ava continued.

By this time, her cheeks turned pink as she wiped tears away from her eyes. She had been called many things in fights with girls in the neighborhood, but she had never been called a thief. This accusation had a particularly harsh sting.

Mrs. Marlaina reached into a manilla folder and handed Ava a photocopy of the check front and back. Ava noted that the check was issued to Heather in the amount of $45.23. *"Really? Why would I steal a forty-five-dollar check when mines be like $500.00 every two weeks?"* Ava thought to herself. She turned her attention to the photo of the back of the check to see the signature line, *"Isla*

Howard," it read in what was clearly her writing. "Mrs. Marlaina," Ava started, "Isla signed the check. This is her writing. Why am I even here? I told you I didn't do this." Ava was confused as ever.

"Her story is that you stole the check from the office here and went to her to make her cash it at one of these corner stores," Mrs. Marlaina said.

"That makes no sense at all! First, I don't have to steal. Second, I would never steal from a disabled person, and third, how in the hell could I force that girl to sign a check in her name and cash it for me?" Ava pleaded to her manager's reason.

"I know it makes no sense Ava. That is why we are investigating until we figure out what happened. We are not firing either of you in the meantime. The two of you are, however, going to be working different shifts. Now, let me make this perfectly clear to you, Ava, you cannot come up here during Isla's shifts, and she is not allowed here during yours. Understood?" Mrs. Marlaina gave Ava a firm look.

"Understood," Ava repeated.

Within hours of leaving Wendy's, Ava started getting calls and text messages from her friends back at her old school. Word was already going around Wilkinsburg High that Ava was a thief. Some chose to believe Isla's story because she was seemingly spoiled. She always had on expensive jewelry, and her mom drove a big truck. That, coupled with the fact that she was petite and pretty, meaning others thought she was above reproach.

After a couple of days of denying rumors and fighting gossip, Ava felt it was time to get to the bottom of things. Isla and Ava had been good friends, so Ava really could not fathom what was going on. The investigation

Wendy's was conducting would probably take forever. Isla had also been ignoring Ava's calls since the incident transpired. Ava knew it was out of guilt. *"I just can't sit around and wait while she gets away with this shit."* Ava thought as she looked at the schedule to see what day Isla worked next.

The wind blew the smell of grilling burgers around the parking lot of Wendy's as Ava went to the front door and pulled the handle. She knew she was not supposed to be on the premises while Isla was there, but she wanted answers. Ava walked past the counter to the fry station, where her eyes met Isla's. Ava started talking in hushed yet urgent whispers to the smaller girl as she approached.

"Why would you make that story up? I got you a job here! We're supposed to be family!" Ava started.

Although Ava kept her voice low, she could see the fear in Isla's eyes. Not only was Isla afraid that Ava was there to fight her, but she was also scared of being outed as a liar.

"Go to hell, you bitch! You know you did that shit!" Isla protested loudly, making a big show by swearing at Ava as loudly as she could. Ava realized that she was intentionally trying to attract attention. Even more shocked and confused by Isla's reaction, Ava stood stunned for a moment.

The crew leader for the shift that evening contacted Mrs. Marlaina and told her what happened. The following day, Ava got a call.

"Ava," Mrs. Marlaina started. "I told you not to bring your behind up here when you were not scheduled to work." Her voice was lined with disappointment. "You been here for years now, Ava. I love you like a daughter, but I have no choice but to let you go. We will mail your last check to you," she finished.

"No! Mrs. Marlaina. I'm sorry! This is so not fair! I did not steal that lady's check," she protested.

"Sorry, but there is nothing I can do about it. The investigation is almost done. I wish you would have just waited as I told you," Mrs. Marlaina said. As Ava hung up the phone, she felt pure anger flowing through her blood stream. There was nothing she could do about what just happened.

About a week later, Wendy's completed their investigation. It was discovered that Isla was the one who stole the check. She was fired immediately. Ava would have been able to keep her job had she not confronted Isla independently. Lesson learned. Given that Ava went to Allderdice now, there was no reason to have contact with Isla or many of the other students she once called friends at Wilkinsburg High. Ava decided just to leave it alone.

***

Spring arrived quickly. Ava had a new job at AJ Wright, a local department store, and was making plans for after high school. First, however, she had to make sure she had everything she needed for the special night, prom. She was going with Yves, who was filled with excitement about the night. The two settled on orange and cream as their colors. Her dress was a floor-length mermaid gown covered in rhinestones. His suit was cream with orange pinstripes. Although Yves would not admit it, he was especially thrilled that his mother said she would meet the couple at Ava's house to see them off.

Yves's mom was a once beautiful and proud Italian woman. Unfortunately, she was introduced to drugs by Yves's father before he was born. As a toddler, he was shuffled between his mom and paternal grandmother's house until one day when he was four. His mother left him at a friend's house and never returned. One of the people in there called his grandmother, who came to get him. She would take care of him as his father was in and out of prison. Yves just started speaking to his mom every now and then in the few months leading up to prom. Ava saw her on the city bus one afternoon on her way to work and invited her over to see them off before they left for prom. His mother accepted eagerly as she informed Ava about how she tried to clean up and be in Yves's life, but his father's side of the family blocked her efforts.

***

"Maybe if I lay on the floor, it will stop hurting so much," Ava said as she winced in pain. She was getting her hair done for the prom, but the excruciating back pain was

95

preventing her from sitting upright in the stylist's chair.

"Girl, what's the matter with you? How are you in this much pain? Did you sleep wrong or something?" the stylist inquired.

"No. Maybe. I don't know," Ava replied. "I just know I have to change positions," she added.

Ava felt a stabbing pain in her back that continued when her mom and Mr. Rich came to pick her up from the hair appointment. Her mom had met Mr. Rich about a month after homecoming. They both worked at Kmart together and had an instant connection. He was a cool dude, different from Brielle's dad, and nothing like the weirdos she tried dating in the past. Ava liked Mr. Rich. She was happy for her mom because she had finally found someone she could build with.

"You can eat, take some pain medicine and get in the bed," Patrice said, confident that the pain would likely subside overnight.

The following morning, Ava could not get out of bed. Her back pain was at a level 10 on the doctor's smiley face pain scale posted in every clinic across America. Her mother helped peel Ava from her mattress and led her to the car for a trip to the emergency room.

"Any history of stomach cancer, kidney failure, hemophilia..." The nurses asked a set of preliminary questions. Ava had no explanation for what could be going wrong with her. "We will run some tests," one of the doctors stated as he ordered blood samples. "I am concerned that you may have a blood clot in your lungs, though," he continued.

"A blood clot!" Patrice repeated, clutching at her chest.

"Do not get too alarmed, ma'am. We will do an x-ray and run some more tests," the doctor said as he eased out of the door.

Just then, Ava's phone began to ring. It was Yves. "Baby, I'm in the hospital. I don't feel good..." Ava started before he interrupted.

"What you mean?" he questioned. "You gone be out by the time prom starts though right?" he continued.

"Umm. I don't know they runnin' tests now," Ava replied, taken aback that Yves sounded more concerned about prom than her health.

"Well, they better hurry up with them shits cause this is my prom, and you have to fuckin come! You cannot mess this night up for me," he started to raise his voice.

"Aww, baby, calm down." Ava tried to soothe him. She did not care much about the

Allderdice prom because it was not "her" school. She would have rather gone to Wilkinsburg's, but she was not allowed to attend.

"I'll see you at the house. You only got a few hours, and I expect you to be there," he said, hanging up before Ava had a chance to respond.

"I have to go. I cannot stay. I need to go to prom," Ava told her mom anxiously. She did not want to miss the prom and disappoint Yves. "Please tell them I have to go."

Patrice looked at Ava with a raised brow. "You could barely even walk here, but you want to go to the prom and dance for hours?" she questioned.

"Yes, mom," Ava pleaded. "This is one night only. If I miss prom, I will regret it for the rest of my life." She embellished the story to appeal to her mother's emotions. Patrice sighed, unaware of the complete lack of sympathy Yves just showed Ava.

"If the doctors say you can go, then fine," she agreed.

"You feel better because you have been given pain medication since you got here." The doctor warned after learning of Ava's intent to check out of the emergency room. "I must tell you, if it is a blood clot causing this symptom and you walk out of here, you could die. You are going to have to sign a waiver refusing any additional treatment against medical advice," he continued.

Ava was still in pain, but she was more mobile than she was when she came in. She felt so much pressure to choose the prom over her health. Ultimately, she checked out and went home to get dressed for the dance.

Ava reached for the knob of her room door. She could hear people in the living room, talking and laughing. Yves arrived about fifteen minutes before Ava was ready. She took a deep breath. She was nervous, and all eyes would be on her in a moment. The adrenaline she felt overshadowed the pain in her back. When Ava emerged from the hallway and walked into the living room, her sister noticed her first.

"Oh, Ava!" she shrieked. "You look so pretty!"

Ava smiled and let her eyes scan the room. They first fell upon Mother, who sat gracefully. A few of her cousins were also there, as well as Mrs. Marlaina and some of Yves's family members, like Aunt Jackie, who raised him after his grandmother died. Mrs. Marlaina and Ava had gotten really close after Ava was proven innocent of the Wendy's check fraud situation. She and Ava bumped heads from time to time, but Ava could tell that Mrs. Marlaina loved her. Ava was also happy to see Yves's mom because she could see the joy in his eyes that came from her presence. The two spent the next twenty minutes taking photos, and it was off to the dance. Despite enjoying her night at prom, Ava had lingering discomfort in her back for the next couple of days that eventually subsided. She never found out what caused the pain she experienced. The only thing she knew for sure was that she was afraid to miss the dance because of the way that Yves was acting.

Chapter 7

Ava clutched her high school diploma as she walked across the stage. She noticed that her Dad, Artie, had shown up with his family, one being her newborn baby brother. *"Oh, now he shows up."* Ava thought to herself. Ava could care less. She felt immense satisfaction at being done with high school. Not only that, she and Yves were planning on getting an apartment together. Every time Ava went to the store, she went to the home goods aisle to look for themes for the bathroom and kitchen. She imagined decorating her place to her liking and not having to answer to her mom.

"I wish the two of you would stop being so stubborn and speak to each other," Mother said. "It just hurts my heart that the two of you do not get along like you should."

The two spoke on the phone regularly. Mother always had the best advice, and as a graduation gift, she gave Ava a couple of hundred dollars to help with a security deposit once she found a place.

"I know," Ava said with a sigh. She decided not to be defensive. After all, there was nothing Ava wanted more than to be closer to her mom. She just did not know how. She decided to change the subject.

"I've been looking at houses in Swissvale," Ava said excitedly.

"Oh yeah?" Mother said. "I remember the first place I got with a couple of roommates in New York," she continued. Ava loved hearing Mother's stories about her modeling days in New York. She listened intently as she told stories of tiny apartments and taking subways to fashion shows.

Ava and Yves moved into a studio basement apartment of a three-unit complex in late August. It was a red-bricked house behind a gas station. At this point, Ava remained working at AJ Wright, while Yves worked at K-Mart. Still, the two would need additional income to cover rent and bills. One day, when Ava was going to get some snacks at the convenience store attached to the gas station, she spotted a "Hiring" sign in the window of the gas station. *"This would be a perfect side hustle,"* Ava thought. *"It's steps away from the house, and it's open 24 hours."* Ava put in an application for both herself and Yves.

Within two weeks, both Ava and Yves were hired to work at the gas station. Ava worked mornings while Yves took the late shifts. Each had two jobs to keep them afloat. All was well for a little while. Amir and Remy came over to visit every weekend. They chilled, played music, and 21 Blackjack together. Ava sometimes fried fish or chicken, while Amir and Remy would bring the drinks and smoke. The pair of couples would get so loud sometimes that George, the old man upstairs, would bang on the floor or come down to their apartment to complain about the noise and smell of smoke coming up to his place from the vents. He was in his late fifties at least, with a head full of gray hair, a tight-fitted tie-dye t-shirt, and black flip flops.

"What y'all doing down here smoking that shit I see," George scolded one Saturday night when he appeared at their door, banging fiercely. He was incredibly bold with his nosiness. "Keep it up! Y'all just keep it up! I'm documenting all of this to tell the landlord! I don't know why you kids feel like y'all are the only ones living around here!"

Yves stood blankly in the doorway while Amir and Remy could barely contain their laughter. "What the hell is his problem?" Remy asked.

"That's just old man George. I think he is going senile or something. He is a drunk too. I see all the beer cans he puts out for recycling every week," Ava responded.

"Damn, dude looks like a snap," Amir observed.

"We don't pay him much mind," Ava said. "He's probably lonely. Nothing better to do than worry about people around him," she added.

Although Ava and Yves both worked two jobs, life was still a struggle sometimes. No one ever taught either of them how to budget or manage money. They would pay their bills, then spend the rest of their money on food, clothes, shoes, and video games, instead of saving or investing. Their money seemed to vanish the same day they were paid. Not only that, Yves worked the bare minimum when it came to hours in favor of having enough time to play video games and hang out with his nephew, who was just two years younger than them. The amount of time Yves spent away from home and not working to keep them from struggling caused tension between him and Ava. Between finances and Yves going missing in action, the pair argued a lot. Arguing soon turned to fights.

"Where are you going? You don't work tonight. It's already midnight," Ava said as she noticed Yves put his phone down and grab his shoes.

"I'm going out with my nephew. Not that it's any of your business," Yves responded.

"Not my business?" Ava said, folding her arms. "It is my damn business. Are you going out with Davon, or are you going to see one of those lil bitches you be texting?" Ava said firmly. She recently discovered that he was still talking to

Shantell, one of the girls he used to flirt with when they were in high school.

"Don't fuckin start with me, Ava," Yves spat.

"Who do you think you are talking to like that?" Ava said.

"Whatever." Yves grabbed his jacket and headed out the door swiftly.

Arguments between the two were happening more frequently. He would talk to girls on the internet and through text. One of the friends Ava met while working at the gas station told her that Yves constantly flirted with attractive girls that stopped in and came to his register. The tension between Ava and Yves continued to build.

Ava looked at the clock as she heard the key unlocking the door to the apartment. It was 9:30 a.m. Yves was out all night, and Ava was livid.

"Where you been?" Ava questioned. Yves collapsed on the couch. He smelled like alcohol and smoke. He sat silently. "I asked where you been. It's all the way the next damn day. You haven't responded to any of my calls or texts. Your ass was not with your nephew." Ava accused.

"Shut ya ass up!" Yves snapped. "I'm tired of your mouth. I told you last night where I was going," Yves added angrily.

Ava had no plans of stopping. "You ain't shit! You hardly work, you play video games all the damn time, and you can't do shit by yourself…" Ava continued to hurl insults while Yves started threatening to smack Ava in the mouth. "You ain't gone hit shit!" Ava said, nearly daring Yves to do just that after he made the remark.

Ava grabbed at Yves's phone when he hit her in the face sending Ava falling back into a side table. That was the first time he had ever hit her, and it would definitely not be the last. He did not stop there. He stood over her and continued to punch and swear at her.

"Stop!" she yelled, trying to block the blows. "Stop! Stop Yves!" she yelled.

Just then, there came a banging from the door to their basement apartment. "Y'all down here beating each other's asses, I hear," called George from the hallway. "I'm calling the police on you ass holes."

Yves stopped hitting Ava when he heard the word police. He looked at his fist, then at Ava balled up on the living room floor crying. Heavily panting, he grabbed his phone and a couple of other personal items to put in a drawstring Nike bag and left the house. Adrenaline flowed through Ava's body. She immediately felt pain on the left side of her face. It was swelling quickly. As she stood up to head to the bathroom, she noticed multiple parts of her body were in pain. Looking in the mirror, Ava found marks on her back and arms where Yves hit her. She also had a large mark on her hip from falling into the end table. She stood shaking and crying for a few moments.

"Mom," Ava said with an unsteady voice. Patrice was the first person Ava thought to call after the incident. "Yves just beat me up," she continued as she started crying again.

"He beat you up?" Patrice said, confusion in her voice.

"He hit me all in my face," Ava added, sobbing. There was a pause on both ends of the line.

"Well, what did you do, Ava? You know you got a smart-ass mouth," Patrice said flatly.

Ava stood stunned. That was not the reaction she was expecting from her mom. *Does it matter what I did? He put his hands on me,* Ava thought. "He was out all night, and we got into it," Ava told her mother. "We got into an argument, and he hit me," she continued.

"I'm sorry that happened to you, Ava, but what do you want me to do? Come beat him up? You ran your ass out of here to go live with him just as soon as you graduated. Welcome to adulthood." Ava hung up the phone without saying goodbye. She gently wiped the tears from her face.

If Ava could not get comfort from her mom, she would find it her own way. She went to the closet, grabbed handfuls of Yves's clothes off hangers, and tossed them out of the front door. She then went outside and doused his belongings with bleach, all the while experiencing spasms of pain where she had been hit.

Later that night, Ava's voicemail box was filled with messages from Yves apologizing for what happened. "Ava, I was drinking. I had too much. I had a damn headache, and you wouldn't shut up," one said. "Hey Ava, it's me; answer the phone. I'm sorry. Damn what you want me to say," said a second. "I love you, Ava, come on. I gotta get my stuff for work."

The messages continued one after another. Ava had to take the day off work. She had to get the swelling on her face to go down, otherwise, it made no difference how much concealer she used.

"You gave me a black eye." Ava finally responded to one of Yves's texts.

"Let me just come to talk to you," Yves pleaded. Ava did not respond.

After a few days, Ava allowed Yves to return to their apartment. He begged Ava for forgiveness, promising that he would never hit her again. It would only be a matter of weeks until their disagreements escalated to physical aggression once again. His anger issues fueled Ava's in return. Yves was mean, communicating in threats and aggression. When his mother died that November, Yves went into a serious depression. He skipped work, slept all day, and drank all night. He started staying out later and more frequently. When Ava would ask him to do something around the house, he would get angry.

At first, Ava tried her best not to fight or argue with Yves, especially after his mother passed. However, when things continued to escalate, Ava started hitting back. He continued with the girls and violent outbursts for some time. Ava suspected Yves was bipolar, but he denied it and never acknowledged that he had any issues.

"Yves, s-s-stop," Ava managed to whisper in between breaths while gasping for air.

Yves had his hand wrapped around Ava's throat. She looked into his eyes, filled with rage. He loosened his grip, and Ava fell to the floor. The two were arguing over nude photos of a random girl Ava found in Yves's phone. Apparently, he considered the act a violation of his privacy.

"Get out!" Ava screamed. She was terrified, holding her neck in disbelief. "*Was he trying to kill me*?" she thought. Yves backed up, looking at his hands. He knew he had gone too far this time. He silently grabbed as many of his things as he could as he waited for Davon to come to pick him up yet again. Hot tears fell from Ava's face. It hurt so badly to swallow. Her throat felt tender, which meant more bruises to hide.

Three weeks went by as Ava worked to put the relationship between her and Yves in the past. He called and texted daily, trying to speak with her, but she refused to answer. He had even tried to get Remy to convince her to let him come back home, but it was no use. Ava was already trying to figure out how she could afford the place without him. She picked up extra shifts at work when she could. Although Ava was hurt, she was proud of herself for making the decision to stay away from him.

As Ava walked down the block of her old neighborhood in Wilkinsburg, a car pulled up beside her. After one glance, she could see it was Yves. "*Shit!*" She thought to herself. She felt a flood of emotions from fear to anger, to love. Whatever the case, Ava was not ready to speak to him.

"Go away!" she yelled as he rolled the window down to speak to her.

"Ava, stop! Let me talk to you!" he pleaded. He parked the car and ran out to catch up with Ava. "I love you, and I want to be with you," he said. "I'm sorry. I'll do whatever you want. Come on, Ava. You know things been hard for me since my mom's passed." He reached out to hug Ava.

"Let me go, Yves," Ava requested. She was confused. She missed him, but she was tired of

115

fighting. She was afraid of him but still loved him. Ava fought back the tears as she listened to him beg.

"Ugh. You again," said George, as he passed through the back door on his way out of the apartment building. Yves had bags in his hand as he made his way inside to bring his things in. It had been a week since he saw Ava walking down the street. He managed to convince her to let him back into the apartment. "Finally got some peace and quiet with you gone, and now here your ass come back to fight I see," he continued.

"Hello, George," Yves said as he moved past the elderly man. "Aye, man, why don't you mind your own damn business?" Yves stopped being offended long ago by his judgments. After all, he never actually called the police as he threatened.

Over the next couple of months, Ava and Yves started to struggle even more financially. Yves still worked as little as he could while spending money on video games. They managed to pay rent on time, but there was little left for other essentials. One day Yves came home with a few things from the gas station and placed them on the counter.

"Why did you get this stuff from the gas station? You know it's cheaper at the Dollar Tree," Ava asked knowing, the mark up at the gas station for basic products was outrageous. She could tell from the yellow price stickers that it all came from their job.

"I just took it," Yves responded. Ava's eyes widened. "It makes sense, doesn't it? We work for the place; we can take a damn tube of toothpaste. They pure profit over there," he continued, not taking his eyes from Grand Theft Auto.

Ava simply shrugged her shoulders. It was just toothpaste and toilet paper. They needed these things, after all. It was not a topic she wanted to get into an argument about. In fact, over the next few weeks, both Ava and Yves started taking items from the gas station here and there. Sometimes it was soap, or milk, or canned goods.

All was well until too much inventory went missing, and management became suspicious.

One day when Ava showed up to work, the owners were present, along with the local police department. Ava was informed that they had video footage of both her and Yves taking items without paying. Yves, who was home at the time, was called in and informed that they would both be charged with retail theft. Ava panicked at the thought of a criminal record, especially over something so petty. To make matters worse, George heard about the firing from the owners, who he had known for some time since living in the area for so long. He wasted no time telling the landlord what Ava and Yves had done. Within 48 hours of the charges being filed, Ava came home to a notice of eviction on their front door.

According to the landlord, he no longer wanted them living in the apartment. It turned out that while George did not call the police, he had been keeping a running list of grievances against the two, which he gladly submitted once he learned about the charges filed against them. Although Ava and Yves paid their rent on time, they still had until the end of the month to vacate the premises. Ava started to panic. Her options were limited.

Chapter 8

Ava felt nauseous. She figured it was the stress of being evicted that caused her late cycle and upset stomach. Still, she had never felt quite so queasy before. Having her suspicions, she went to the Magee Women's Clinic in Wilkinsburg for a pregnancy test. She sat quietly in the exam room for her results. She was excited and nervous. Ava knew she wanted kids someday, but she was not sure about her relationship with Yves. After all, they just got back together. If he had his anger under control and sought counseling, she would feel safer. Not only that, they had to leave their apartment soon. About five minutes later, the nurse came in with the results.

It was a cold day in February when Ava and Yves went to their court hearing for the charges from the gas station incident. Patrice was there to pick Ava up.

"Thank you for letting us stay with you mom," Ava said.

She was being humble despite never wanting to ask Patrice for anything. Ava took a deep breath. "I have some news for you," she continued. "I'm pregnant."

Patrice stopped dead in her tracks. She was in the middle of putting her seatbelt on when she looked up at Ava. "No, you aren't," she said in disbelief.

"Yeah, I am, actually," Ava replied, unsure what to say next. Patrice did not believe Ava. She was shocked. So much so that the two went to the store for an at home test despite Ava telling her mom that she went to the clinic. Patrice wanted her own confirmation.

"I have some information for you to Ava," Patrice said after Ava had taken the test, solidifying the information she was told just an hour before. Ava looked up at her mom intently as they sat at the kitchen table. "Mother is sick," Patrice said.

"I know," Ava responded. "I already know about the lung cancer and the treatment and everything," she added.

121

"No, Ava." Patrice shook her head. "She is extremely sick. Her health is fading fast. The doctors said she has 3 to 6 months at the most," she said, tears gathering in her eyes. Ava and her grandmother spoke often.

Their conversation was always pleasant. They listened and laughed with each other. However, Ava did not know quite how ill Mother had been. Three to six months was no time at all. She needed time to spend with Ava's child once he or she was born. This was not supposed to be happening. Not now. Ava buried her head in her hands and began to weep.

About two months after Ava and Yves moved in with Patrice, Mother came to stay as well. Her health deteriorated rapidly. She was in pain constantly and losing weight fast, as she was not eating regularly. Sometimes, she would even become delusional. Vonte was not able to take care of Mother on his own at her house, so he, along with Ava and Patrice, took turns staying in the room set up for her comfort. During this time, the resentment between Ava and her mom died down as the focus was taking care of the ailing matriarch. Although Brielle was still too young to care for Mother on her own, the two sat talking and telling each other jokes during the times Mother was coherent. It was hard to tell what she was actually able to process.

Yves could not contain his anger despite living under Patrice's roof. He still had not seen a doctor as promised and was meaner than ever. At the time, Yves still was not making much money, going from one temp agency to another. Currently, he was doing home healthcare as a nursing assistant. Still, he managed to flirt with the girl he was scheduled to partner with when he had to go on assignments. This led to more fighting. "I'm pregnant, for goodness sake Yves!" Ava yelled at him after finding messages in his phone yet again.

One day, while Patrice was a work, Yves and Ava got into an argument while Vonte was over the house. Having no idea that the two fought as they did, he stepped in to intervene.

"I don't really give a shit what the two of ya'll got going on, but my grandmother is in the other room sick, for crying out loud! Ya'll need to stop this shit now!" Vonte scolded them both from the kitchen.

Yves snapped from the bedroom he shared with Ava, "I don't give a fuck!" loud enough to wake Mother from her sleep.

Vonte and Ava were furious. "You can get your freeloading, bum ass out of my mom's house if you have a problem!" Vonte asserted.

Yves ran into the kitchen to find where the harsh words came from. Ava raced behind him, trying to catch him before he confronted her brother. Once the two got near each other, they started fighting immediately. They scuffled as Ava cried for them to stop. Mother was fully aware of what was going on.

"Ya'll need to stop! Please!" Mother cried from her room.

Ava was hysterical as she struggled to pull the two apart. "She can hear ya'll please! Y'all making it worse!" She managed to wedge herself between the two and demanded that Yves go take a walk. Yves stood, looking at his hands again. His anger had seized his senses. "Go take a walk," Ava said firmly, breathing heavily as she looked at Vonte. Yves grabbed his shoes and phone, speaking to no one as he made his way out the door.

"Yo, what the hell was that?" Vonte looked at Ava with disgust on his face. Ava did not have a ready response, so she began tidying the kitchen silently.

Ava, Patrice, Vonte, and Brielle continued to take turns talking and sitting with Mother. "Mommy, Ava is pregnant," Patrice informed her mother as the two sat together. Mother's eyes lit up. She was so happy to hear the news. At this point, none of them could tell whether Mother really understood or not. She just was not quite the same person anymore. She did respond with clarity at Patrice's statement, however.

"That is going to be a beautiful boy with pretty eyes," she said. This interested Patrice greatly because, at this point, the sex of the baby was still unknown.

It was a Sunday evening in the dead of summer. Ava and Yves were in their room talking. Vonte was in the kitchen, and Patrice had just gotten up from talking to Mother. Brielle came in at sundown from playing with the neighborhood kids. She went right into her grandmother's room to check on her, just like she had been doing for the past few months.

"Mommy!" Brielle yelled at the top of her lungs. "Mommy! Grandma is not breathing!"

Everyone in the house ran to the room where Mother was previously sleeping and confirmed that she was gone. "She waited until we were all here to take her last breath," Patrice said with conviction. "I was literally just in here moments before."

Mother died on July 26, 2009. She had become so fragile and thin that her clothes would not fit. When the coroner came, they all watched and wept as her lifeless body was taken from their home. No one got any sleep that night. They each stayed up crying, and reminiscing on the good times they shared with her.

The night before the service, Ava, Patrice, and Brielle went to the funeral home to do Mother's makeup, nails, and hair. Ava made a wig for her that she had never worn before, and Patrice insisted that she be buried in the beautiful pink silk pajama set with varying shades of pink flowers that Ava had gotten her for Christmas the year prior. They took a moment to cry one last time while embracing in an endless hug. Mother still had the grace and beauty of a model through to her final days. The casket was closed for the funeral. Only the immediate family got to view her body for the last time. Mother would never have anyone looking down on her, even in death.

Funerals have a way of bringing back people and problems of the past. Ava's Aunt Nicky came to town from Leechburg with her long-time girlfriend. "I can't believe she had the nerve to show her face after all this time. She didn't even have the decency to come to visit or help when her own mother was sick." Patrice shot daggers through her eyes.

Ava's aunt was about five years older than her mom. Years prior, she saw her aunt on a regular basis. She always seemed to have serious issues with her girlfriend that she would put onto her grandmother. That angered Patrice as she saw how much stress it put on her mother. Patrice decided to distance herself from her sister. Things got even worse one year when Nicky let her son co-sign for a car for Patrice. When the two sisters got into an argument over Mother, Nicky came and took the car from Patrice out of spite. Even with the car no longer in Patrice's possession, Nicky still demanded that Patrice make the car payments. When Patrice refused, the two stopped speaking. "*You came and took the car. What the hell kind of sense does that make?*" Ava recalled her mother screaming into the phone. That was their last conversation as far as Ava knew.

"Yves? That's not even her grandson," Nicky said, loud enough for Ava and Patrice to hear from the pew behind them.

With all the seating available, Nicky still managed to sit near them. Ava rubbed her stomach. Nicky did not even know she was pregnant. Nicky had not been around, so she knew nothing of Yves. They were so out of touch. The comment came after the Reverend read the obituary. The name "Yves" appeared as a grandson. Patrice included Yves because he had been there helping with Mother along with us. He spent countless hours near her bedside crying and talking to her. Yves loved Mother like she was his own grandmother. *Being petty in a funeral home,*" Ava thought to herself. *"I just cannot believe it, the nerve of her."*

During the service, the funeral director covered Mother's casket with a white blanket that had an angel on the front. A friend of Ava's aunt sent it from Leechburg. The intent was that she be buried with it, covering her for eternity. However, Patrice and Ava were shocked to learn that Nicky took it for herself shortly after the preacher stopped talking. Nicky then went straight back home to Leechburg, without saying goodbye or going to the repast. That was the last time Patrice and Ava heard or saw Nicky for years. Ava never forgot the hurt in her mom's eyes as she saw her mother's casket being lowered into the ground without the angel to protect her on her journey. *"Lesson learned,"* Ava thought to herself, yet again. *"Some people just don't care how shitty they are."*

Chapter 9

Ava went in for a routine prenatal appointment on September 15, 2009. She had to go in to see her doctor more often late in her pregnancy because the baby was due soon, and she had developed preeclampsia early on in her pregnancy, which caused for even more precautions. The swelling in her hands and feet was becoming unbearable. When the doctor looked at her vitals, he informed Ava that they would have to induce her labor. When she heard the news, her mind began to race. It was earlier than expected, by three weeks, to be precise. Yves was at work, and she had their only car. Ava called Patrice, who agreed to pick Yves up before heading to the hospital.

Around 4:00 p.m., Yves, Brielle, Mr. Rich, and Patrice arrived at the hospital. Ava was already in a birthing room dressed in a hospital gown. The hours passed slowly as Ava shifted on the bed in pain. She had an epidural to ease the contractions, but the night was still difficult. It was over 12 hours since she was induced, and Ava had yet to dilate. By 6:00 a.m. the following day, the doctors gave her more news. "At this point," one of the doctors said, "You are going to need to have a cesarean. The baby's heart rate keeps rising and falling from the stress of labor."

Ava did not want a c-section, but doctors left her with no choice. Besides, she was exhausted mentally and physically already from tossing and turning all night with a monitor attached to her. The staff wheeled her to the operating room for the procedure. Yves followed closely behind. "Wait here," one of the nurses instructed Yves.

The doctors and nurses were talking about whatever song was playing on the radio as they prepped Ava's stomach. They were comfortable, clearly having done this countless times before. Meanwhile, Ava was tired, scared, and emotional. She laid flat on her back, trying to avoid staring directly into the blinding lights overhead. Her arms were tied down to the table as a standard precaution. It seemed reasonable to Ava because she was close to panicking and running out of the room, not that she would get very far. Moments later, Yves appeared at Ava's side. As the doctor asked for the scalpel, Ava

132

started to feel sick. Her head started spinning. She was so heavily sedated; it was hard for her to speak.

"Throw up" was all she could manage to whisper. Yves was busy looking around the operating room. There were a number of shiny metal instruments on the table next to the doctor. He looked at Ava when he noticed her mouth moving.

"What did you say, babe?" He leaned down to her.

She took a breath. "Throw up," she repeated.

"You're going to spit up?" Yves asked, alarmed. Ava nodded her head, yes, gently. "I need something! She's going to throw up!" he said to one of the least busy looking nurses. Someone handed him a small plastic pan.

"You're going to have to tilt her head over to the side so she does not choke," one nurse said, unable to leave her position next to the doctor.

Yves did as he was told, just in time for Ava to expel what little fluid she had on her stomach. She felt terribly sick, fearing she would pass out. Just then, Ava felt a weight being lifted. "One beautiful baby boy!" the doctor said as he held the baby up high enough for a nurse to cut the umbilical cord.

On September 16, 2009, Yves D. Jeffries II was born, weighing 6 pounds, 9 ounces. Ava never knew a love like what she experienced that day. Her newborn was so tiny, gentle, and pure. It gave her hope for a new beginning.

A month later, Ava sat in an old wooden rocking chair in the corner of her room at Patrice's house. She gazed out of the only window the room had to offer. There was a crib along the only empty wall. Her son slept quietly in her arms as she thought about the past year. Ava and Yves's relationship was still rocky. She prayed that things would get better now that there was a child in the picture. Ava knew she put up with a lot of hurtful behavior from Yves because she felt bad that he had been dealt such a difficult hand in life. Ava knew that the void left by his parents affected him in many ways. Not to mention the abuse he suffered at the hands of family members who were supposed to be looking out for him. Still, Ava didn't know if that was a good enough excuse for the way he treated her. She just wanted to focus on getting back on their feet and out of Patrice's house while Yves was more concerned with cheating, lying, and hanging out with his friends. She was uncertain about the future but continued to pray and have faith that life would be better for her son, for their family. Yves was happy when junior was born. So maybe, just maybe, he would get his act together and change his ways.

Ava realized that her lifestyle with Yves could teach Junior how to survive, not how to thrive. Ava promised that her parenting would be different than what she experienced growing up. "Don't you worry, little baby," she said to her sleeping child. "You are loved. I'm going to tell you everything you need to know about how to navigate through this world. I am here to help you and guide you. Just know that you can come to talk to me about any and everything," she said as she kissed his little forehead. "You are going

135

to be a strong, confident little boy who works hard and is kind to others. I will be there. I will be involved. I am ready to listen," she promised. "Family is all we have," Ava continued. Mother's death added depth and perspective to how short life can be.

At that moment, Ava experienced peace and self-acceptance. She realized that she had been looking for love and answers in all of the wrong places. Trauma was not Living. Growing up too fast was not ideal. Ava knew that the fighting between her and Yves would only harm their child. She decided to have an honest talk with Yves and give him an ultimatum. He would either have to make a pledge to be the best possible person he could be, or their relationship would have to come to an end. Ava's true journey would begin that day as she made the commitment to love herself and her son above all others.

Ava closed her eyes and continued to reflect. *"When you feel that you are lacking support and love from family, you go looking for it elsewhere. You get mixed up in situations."* She thought as she considered the fights and suspensions, she had in school growing up. *"I let a lot of things happen to me because I just did not know any better. I did not have the confidence to stand up for myself. Over the years, I got used to people hurting me, starting with my dad, who abandoned me and distanced himself further away from me as my siblings continued being born, and my mom who was always so indifferent."* Ava continued to ponder as she looked out of the window, up to the blue sky above. The relationship Ava had with Patrice still had its ups and downs, but they were supporting one another through their grievances. Patrice was head over heels in love with junior too. He came at a time where their hearts were shattered. He shined light, love, and happiness upon them. Patrice started telling Ava stories about Mother when she was younger. Although Ava felt Patrice was not there for her during her teenage years, yet she was grateful that she was going out of her way to help with her new grandbaby and giving them a temporary place to stay. Ava just wished communicating, and people were easier to manage.

Chapter 10

My mom, Brielle, and I were out shopping for Yves Jr. on a Saturday afternoon. As we sifted through baby clothes, I looked up and noticed Sin and Keisha walking through the aisles with their thirteen-month-old son. Deep feelings stirred within me. Keisha and I were like best friends when I moved to Wilkinsburg all those years ago, back in the fall of 2001. Sin was one of my first loves. I felt some type of way about them for getting together. I knew Keisha was pregnant and had the baby, but I never actually saw the two of them together until that day.

Keisha and I just sort of stopped being friends one day. Little did I know, it was because she started talking to Sin. I know he and I broke up, but still, what about the girl code? Keisha spent a lot of time at my house, eating my food and hanging out. My mom cared for her like a daughter. Keisha even called my mom, "Ma." Besides that, Sin and I spent a lot of our relationship around Keisha because she was one of my best friends. Now, they were together and had a child that was just over a year older than

138

mine. I did not know how to feel at that moment. A thousand questions swirled around in my head. Was I hurt? Betrayed? Angry? Who was at fault for all this? Him or her? What happened to loyalty?

Keisha and I cut eyes at one another. She patted Sin on the shoulder and pointed in my direction. He and I made eye contact as well, but I decided to keep going about my business. After all, the past was the past, and people are allowed to move on.

After I checked out and made my way to the store entrance, I heard a voice from behind. I looked back to see Keisha approaching. "*What the hell could she possibly want*?" I thought to myself.

"Hey, Ava. It's been a while. Wow," she started.

"Yeah," I said shortly.

"You look great, and what a cute little one," Keisha added while she peaked over into Yves Jr.'s stroller. Patrice looked Keisha up and down

139

disapprovingly and rolled her eyes. "I was wondering if I could get your number. You know, to catch up," Keisha finished.

I took a moment before *responding. "What? This is weird. What do we have to talk about? You have a kid with my ex. Fuck off."* I thought. Instead, I said, "Umm. Okay, whatever…" and proceeded to give her my number.

"Well, that was awkward." My mom pointed out while we were walking to the car.

"Right," I said simply. I did not want her to notice any changes in my voice. There was a lump in my throat from the memories that flashed through my mind so quickly.

As fate would have it, I saw Sin again, just a week later. He ended up coming into the Giant Eagle where I was working and ended up in my line to check out.

"What's up, Ava," he said as he approached the counter. "I didn't think I would see you again so soon," Sin said, flashing his signature grin. "It was really nice to run into you the other day," he added. I felt my stomach flip, still confused about how to feel. We made small talk for a few moments while I checked his items out.

When I got to the break room, I checked my phone as usual. I had a message from an unknown number that read, *"Hey, I just wanted you to know that I still love you. I never stopped loving you, Ava."* My heart skipped a beat. I replied to the text even though I was certain who the sender was. *"Who is this*?" I inquired. After a few moments, my phone buzzed with another message. *"Your old bae, Sin."* I smiled involuntarily.

What was I supposed to do with that revelation? I was still involved with Yves and just had a baby not too long ago. Still, the way my heart was beating told me I still had feelings for Sin, who was, by the way, with Keisha. The entire situation was complicated. I took a moment to come up with a well thought out reply and pressed, "Send."

REMINISCENCE

CPSIA information can be obtained
at www.ICGtesting.com
Printed in the USA
LVHW091642100221
678949LV00003B/502